Hickory Doc's Tales

THE PACK: FIRST GENERATION

Hickory Doc's Tales

LINDA HARKEY

ARCHWAY
PUBLISHING

Archway Publishing books may be ordered
through booksellers or by contacting:

Archway Publishing
1663 Liberty Drive
Bloomington, IN 47403
www.archwaypublishing.com
1 (888) 242-5904

Because of the dynamic nature of the Internet, any web addresses or
links contained in this book may have changed since publication and
may no longer be valid. The views expressed in this work are solely those
of the author and do not necessarily reflect the views of the publisher,
and the publisher hereby disclaims any responsibility for them.

Any people depicted in stock imagery provided by Thinkstock are
models, and such images are being used for illustrative purposes only.
Certain stock imagery © Thinkstock.

ISBN: 978-1-4808-4725-5 (sc)
ISBN: 978-1-4808-4723-1 (hc)
ISBN: 978-1-4808-4724-8 (e)

Library of Congress Control Number: 2017909379

Print information available on the last page.

Archway Publishing rev. date: 6/30/2017

CONTENTS

CHAPTER 1

The Black-Hearted Hunter

WESTWARD HO

I am the oldest and wisest in my family of five dogs. We call our kennels the Lazy Dog Hacienda. We live on Shorthair Boulevard in Oklahoma.

Folks around here call me Doc. I tolerate that, but my official name is Chicoree's Hickory Doc. You can trace my family tree back to a sapling in Germany.

My great-great-great-grandpa, Esser's Chic, was a champion hunting dog in Germany who longed for excitement and adventure. He headed West by boat, carrying his blanket and a favorite chow bowl. His plan was to hunt birds with his cousin Wolfsjaeger in Canada. However, our destiny changed when my grandpa saw the Statue of Liberty and realized he was in America!

People in America called our breed German shorthaired pointers. My pa, Chicoree's Doc, said there were three reasons for that. We were from Germany, had short-haired coats, and pointed and retrieved birds on land and water.

So as you can see, my breed is known for hunting. My coat is shiny, short, and liver (a brown color). It's definitely not the kind of liver you eat.

My tail is docked. That's a fancy word for a cutoff tail. It's the size of a rawhide roll.

My annoying younger brother Windwalker Storm Shadow—better known as Zeke—has duller hair that is a ticked color (speckled liver and white). His eyes have a shifty, suspicious appearance as if he has done something he shouldn't have.

Personally, I've always felt that ticked dogs consider themselves to have a better pedigree than the rest of us. The "Storm Shadow" part of Zeke's name really fits him. Zeke usually shakes his body when he is mad or when he's scared of the storms we have in Oklahoma. At the same time Zeke does that, his teeth chatter, which is quite a feat since they are worn down to little nubs from years of chewing on wire fences and kennel runs. He likes to get sympathy from people. Zeke is the most selfish and generally annoying dog in our kennel.

I could give you many examples of my brother's weird personality, but that would take up my entire story. So I'll just tell you a couple.

Once Zeke trotted up to me and said, "Doc, only ticked dogs have nobility and royal blood."

"How do you figure that?" I barked. "We're *brothers*! Remember?"

"Yes, but you have a common liver coat, probably from the *peasant* side of the family. I, on the other hand, have a regal-looking coat."

Or take the time when we all got McDonald's French fries from our people. Zeke gobbled his down, pushed me aside, and finished mine.

"Why did you do that, Zeke?" I growled. "I wasn't finished eating mine."

"Doc," Zeke said, glaring. "I'm younger and need

more food to keep my strength up for hunting season."

As I said, Zeke and I are as different as cats and dogs. Since I'm the oldest, I try to keep him in line. That's definitely a full-time job. Bad Zeke often comes out, especially when he wants something—usually something that I have.

However, Zeke and I do have one thing in common, namely our love of Patch, my daughter. She looks like me only smaller. Her official name is Jayhawk Crow Patch. She was given this name at birth because blue jays, hawks, and crows flew over her.

Ma once said, "Doc, if birds fly over pups when they are born, that means that the pups will become great hunting dogs." Ma was right. Patch finds quail coveys better than any of us.

PRICKLY CHOLLA CACTUS

Now that you know something about us, let me tell you the great story about the black-hearted hunter. It started many hunting seasons ago.

Zeke, Patch, and I were hunting quail in the

canyons. We were with our hunter, better known as the great one. A perilous situation arose on the last afternoon of our hunting weekend. We stopped by a group of live oak trees on the top of the canyon ridge.

Bad Zeke started to whine, "Doc, I'm tired of going up and down the canyon. Dogs of nobility should not have to work this hard! Why can't we hunt on flat land or go home?"

Disgusted, I barked, "Zeke, this is the only way to find quail today. Patch and I worked hard, but you don't hear us complaining."

"Yes, but you are not of *nobility*. I should be directing the work, not actually doing it!"

Suddenly, the wind blew harder, and the sun disappeared behind the clouds. I raised my head and sniffed the air. It smelled damp. The clouds changed to a dark gray. Rain began pouring from the sky. Zeke, our weather dog, started trembling and shaking. *Click-clack, click-clack* sounded as Zeke's teeth hit together. This meant only one thing. A storm was coming!

A bolt of lightning struck the oak tree closest to Zeke. Then we heard the sound of thunder—*boom, bang, boom!* Zeke jumped so high I thought a rocket ship had launched. He didn't land back on the launch pad. Nope, my brother landed on a clump of prickly cholla cactus. The thorns of the cactus sank into Zeke like paws into mud. He let out the loudest shriek I've ever heard, hopping around with the cactus attached to his rump.

I barked, "Zeke, where is your nobility now?" Just as I said that, we heard thunder again.

I glanced at Zeke and then at the dark sky. "Zeke, I'll bet you don't know what has hold of you. It's called a jumping cholla cactus. I haven't seen one this big in years. You'll have to hold still while our hunter gets it out of your coat."

Zeke stopped in his tracks. He hung his head low while the hunter picked the cactus out of his body with needle-nose pliers. People always brought them on hunting trips just for situations like this. The wind started blowing hard and began moving the cholla cactus needles away. Even the cactus didn't want to be around Zeke.

We heard our hunter say, "There's a big storm coming. We need to head back to the trailer. We've had a good day, but Zeke, you look tired."

I barked, "People always blame us when they're the ones who are tired. It looks like you got your wish, Zeke. We're headed back to the trailer."

ROTTEN EGGS AND THE DISAPPEARANCE OF PATCH

We started back. I smelled rotten eggs as the wind picked up and raindrops fell. Then Zeke and I started running when we heard the sound of thunder again. The rotten egg smell went away. It had been four hunting seasons since I had noticed that smell. It reminded me of the hunter who scared all hunting dogs—Big Bad Carl!

Big Bad Carl was known as the meanest, nastiest hunter in the state. The animals said that he was big and strong and that he had a black heart because he was raised by a grizzly bear. Big Bad Carl had long, unkempt, shoulder-length black hair and a stubbly black beard filled with dirt and leaves. He had dark, beady eyes. But worst of all, Big Bad Carl smelled like rotten eggs. He would steal German shorthaired pointers, barely feed and water them, and use them the remainder of the bird season. When hunting season was over, he would dump them in the woods, and they would have to fend for themselves.

The sound of thunder and hard rain drew my attention back to our situation. We started running back to the trailer with our hunter in front. Zeke and I were in the middle, and Patch was behind us. The tree limbs swung back and forth. The rain blinded us from seeing anything, front or back!

Zeke and I completed the journey down the side of the canyon wall just as the rain subsided. Our hunter was still ahead of us on the gravel road when Zeke barked, "Doc, where is Patch? I don't see her behind us."

I turned around. "You're right. This isn't like her. She always stays close to us. I have a bad feeling."

"Don't worry, Doc. I'll find her!" Zeke started running back up the canyon wall. I followed Zeke. I couldn't believe how fast Zeke ran. This was the only time I remembered him running this fast and showing any concern for another dog. It was actually hard to keep up with my brother.

We traveled through thick brush and trees. We

journeyed up the canyon wall and then straight across and down again to the gravel road. Zeke barked in the distance. His bark grew louder and more intense as we came closer. The smell of rotten eggs grew stronger. Then we found them!

WATER AND A PICKUP TRUCK

The rotten egg smell came from Big Bad Carl. Zeke stood on his hind legs, scratching the driver's side of the truck with his front paws. He growled, barked, and showed his teeth at Big Bad Carl, who sat inside the cab of the truck. The torrential rain had flooded the creek bed earlier and left the truck stuck in mud.

Patch was in the back of the truck. One end of a rope was tied around her neck, and the other was attached in the back of Big Bad Carl's old, brown pickup truck. Her coat was covered in mud and grass. She was trembling.

Big Bad Carl shouted at Zeke, "Get away from here, you ugly dog, before I open this door and knock you down. You can't have her!"

Then Big Bad Carl let out a loud laugh that sounded like a lion's roar. His dark, beady eyes glared down at Zeke. He threw open the door, which sent Zeke backward into the rising water. Zeke dog-paddled back and grabbed Big Bad Carl's water-bloated pant leg with a death grip.

I managed to jump into the back of the pickup truck. "Patch, Patch, don't worry. We'll get you out of this mess! I'm going to bite through the rope."

Patch trembled as she said, "Oh, I was so scared! I thought I would never see you again."

I chewed hard on the rope and then asked, "What happened? How did Big Bad Carl catch you?"

"A squirrel darted beside me in the bushes on our way back to the trailer. I started chasing it. I realized too late it was a stuffed squirrel on top of Big Bad Carl's hat! He reached for me, grabbed me by my collar, and tied this rope around my neck. Thank goodness Uncle Zeke chased us to this low water crossing!"

After saying all this, Patch let out a long sigh and started sobbing. I licked her across the face and continued gnawing at the rope. The people caught up with us and started helping Zeke wrestle with Big Bad Carl.

Suddenly, the truck started moving. We were beginning to slide slightly to one side. I was worried the pickup truck would turn over and float away. Patch would drown if I didn't get her out of there fast! There was only one thing to do—get the attention of the others. I started howling and barking.

ZEKE SAVES THE DAY

Zeke finally let go of the *death grip* and paddled to the bed of the pickup truck. It took only one *huge* leap for him to land in the back. Zeke's posturing to look dignified was gone. His coat was matted with mud, and he looked like a common stray dog. But Zeke was determined as he bit down on the rope. Within a few seconds, he completed the task. Patch was free! I guess all those hunting seasons of biting on barbed wire really paid off.

Zeke panted and asked, "Are you all right, Patch?"

She nodded. At this point, Zeke, Patch, and I realized we were in serious danger. The truck was about to turn over. Zeke barked, "Follow me." We jumped off the truck and paddled to shore.

In the meantime, Big Bad Carl had worked his way free from our hunter. Our hunter had pulled him halfway out of the cab, but he had managed to get back in the cab and shut the door. The water continued to rise. The truck turned over with him inside and floated down the rain-swollen creek bed. That was the last time we saw Big Bad Carl.

We were glad to get back to the kennels and home. We received extra pats on the head and our favorite dog treats, *pig ears*! Our hunter was proud of us. Later Patch whispered, "Pa, you know how we talk about *bad* Uncle Zeke. Well, today only *good* Uncle Zeke was there. He was unselfish, and he saved my life!"

I nodded and said, "Your uncle Zeke is a dog of many surprises. Perhaps we have always assumed he would act badly in any situation. This goes to prove that any dog can change its colors if given the right circumstances. Maybe your uncle Zeke has been around us so long we are beginning to bring out the best in him." I wasn't sure what to make of my brother's actions, but this day was his *finest*!

CHAPTER 2

The Long and Short of It

NEWT'S TAIL

"Looking glass, looking glass, what do I see? I see only me!"

After I uttered those words, Zeke, trembled. "Not the barn again. We're not going to the barn! I just won't have it. You know how upset I get. It ... it frightens me, Doc."

Patch barked as her eyes darted between Zeke and me. "Pa, Uncle Zeke is scaring me. Why does Newt have to say *those* words when he sees the looking glass? Why do we have to go with him to the barn?"

"My dear Patch, those words have been handed down from generation to generation to all hunting dogs at the Lazy Dog Hacienda. Hunting dogs must go and see the looking glass in the barn when they reach the age of two. Newt is two. Tradition says his family must be with him. Don't be frightened. That's just your uncle Zeke talking."

"I'm ready to go, Doc." Newt jumped and twisted his body around, wagging his tail from side to side. "I'm not afraid of the barn. This will be fun. You bet it will be. Come on, guys. Let's go."

Newt is very different from us, even though we still consider him part of our family. He is longer and taller than the rest of us with a coat that is thick, shiny, and black. Newt has the most unusual tail. It is very long—not short like ours. Newt is what the people call a Labrador retriever. Labradors have the job of hunting, and finding and retrieving (bringing back to the people) ducks, geese, doves, pheasants, and grouse in water and on land. Our main job is hunting, finding, and retrieving quail and grouse on land. Although German shorthaired pointers have webbed feet and can swim in water to retrieve birds, some consider it to be beneath us. Zeke always says, "Only the common hunting dogs get in water."

Newt accidently hit Zeke squarely in the face with his wagging tail. The blows were hard—*whack, whack, thud.* What a sight! Zeke sprawled flat on the ground, and Newt looked puzzled. All of us started barking and howling—except, of course, my brother, Zeke, who gave a few short growls while struggling to stand. Zeke always made a big deal of any injustice *he* thought someone had done to him.

Not happy at all, Zeke barked, "That is the last time your *furry, long tail* is going to hit me! It's time for me, the smartest of all hunting dogs, to tell you about your pedigree!"

"Zeke, I'm warning you. Don't say another word. Remember, all truths will come when Newt faces the looking glass," I replied.

"Zeke, what does *pedigree* mean?" Newt asked as he promptly sat down in the nastiest and filthiest puddle of water in the whole north pasture. Newt usually finished that off with rolling back and forth on his back so that all the grass would stick to his coat. Then he liked to run through the doggy door in the garage to make sure he left parts of grass, leaves, sticks, and unmentionables for the people. But today that part would have to wait. Taking Newt to the barn was much more important.

Zeke rose to his most dignified pose, sitting straight up with his head up and giving the nobility stare. "Newt, the word *pedigree* means the line of our ancestors, which shows *we* are purebred animals. We are purebred German shorthaired pointers. Why, we even have papers that say so, and the people keep those locked up. That's how *important* we are! But *you*, Newt—"

"Stop that right now, Zeke!" I growled and then curled the part of my upper lip that showed my longest, whitest teeth. Zeke always backed down when I stood tall, growled, and curled the lip.

Zeke looked away before mumbling, "Well, I guess Doc *might* be right this time. You will find out at the looking glass. Let's get going."

A PINK DOG

We marched toward the barn. I was first. Patch and Newt were in the middle. Zeke was moving slowly like a turtle and was pulling up the rear. He said it gave him time to think about all the "dog eat dog" problems in the world. I knew better. He believed being at the rear would protect him from any problems we might find along the way.

The barn was brown. The four horse stalls were open on one end while the rest of the barn was enclosed. And today the horses were all out munching on the prairie grass.

I noticed the side door was opened slightly. I stopped abruptly to nudge the door with my nose. That's the great thing about being German short-haired pointers. We have long noses! Our noses are good for smelling, nudging other dogs and people, and getting into the barn. Patch ran into me, which caused what people called "a domino effect." Newt ran into Patch, and Zeke ran into Newt's wagging tail. The only sounds I heard were *whack, whack, thud.* I turned around. Zeke was on the ground. He was so mad his ticked color had turned pink. Yes, pink! No one could tell what would happen when a ticked dog got mad.

"Newt, you did it again!" Zeke yelped.

"Zeke, I'm sorry. You know I didn't do it on purpose. I can't figure out why my tail hits things. The rest of you don't seem to have that problem." Newt looked pitiful and bowed his head.

"Well, don't let it happen again," Zeke growled.

"We don't have time for all that bickering, Zeke. The looking glass is calling us." I tried to straighten things out so Zeke would calm down. It required a great deal of patience when dealing with Zeke.

RAWHIDE AND BONES

Slowly, we entered the barn. Patch was amazed by all she saw. She blinked her eyes rapidly. "Pa, what are these *things*?"

"Well, these *things* are what the people consider important. It's like our rawhides and bones that we bury. Only people put their *things* in the barn."

Pausing a moment, I continued, "See the hay for us, the saw horse, the people chairs and tables, the …"

Just then we heard a *crashing* sound. I turned around, and I saw Zeke tangled up in the ladder. Newt hung his head low. "I'm sorry. I didn't realize I was so close to the ladder. I was wagging my tail when—"

"Doc, get Newt to the looking glass before anything else happens!" Zeke growled. The short hairs on his back stood straight up. The hairs on Zeke's back spent so much time in the standing position that I often wonder if they would ever just take off.

Patch and I howled. Zeke's legs were sticking up between the rungs of the ladder. He looked like an upside-down beetle thrashing around.

THE WORDS

As the strongest of the bunch, Newt and I finally raised the ladder up enough so that Zeke could get out from under it. Then we all walked slowly toward the wall that held the looking glass. It was about six pups tall and four pups wide. The border was made out of copper. Copper was one thing even dogs would not chew. It didn't have any taste.

Patch, Zeke, and I backed away from the wall as I barked with authority. "Newt, as you go and face the looking glass, don't forget to say *the words*."

Newt edged up to face the mirror. "Looking glass, looking glass, what do I see? I see only me!" Newt stood peering into the looking glass when suddenly he barked, "Doc, I see my reflection in the mirror, and it's not like yours. I look so different from you. My coat is thicker and longer than yours. My tail, my tail—it's very long. No wonder I keep hitting things." Newt moaned and hung his head low.

"Newt, what's wrong with being different?"

"I don't know, Doc. I just look so different. I always thought I was like all of you. Why do I have such a thick coat?"

"Because you are a Labrador retriever. People take you to hunt birds that fall in water. Your thick and dark coat will keep you warm when you jump in the water to retrieve ducks," I answered as I scratched behind my ears.

"Right, Newt. When it's cold, you stay warmer than us because our coat is short and not as thick," Patch barked.

"What about my long tail? Every time I turn around, I hit Zeke!"

"You can say that again," Zeke growled.

"Wait a minute," I said. "Newt, it would be hard for you to swim without your tail. It's like a rudder on a boat. It helps guide you. You need your tail to swim in the water. Your webbed paws also help you swim.

THE FAMILY

Newt stood taller and faced the looking glass. "I guess this does reflect a true picture of me. There are many good reasons why I'm different from you."

"Right," Patch added. "That makes me who I am and you who you are. We're still a *family*."

Newt nodded. "I am proud of my differences. Now that I know I have a much longer tail than all of you, I'll be able to judge my distance better."

Later Patch pulled me aside and asked, "Pa, why

did Uncle Zeke act so scared when we talked about going to the barn? I really enjoyed it."

"Well, my daughter, the looking glass faithfully reflects a true picture of each dog. Maybe your uncle Zeke was afraid to look in the glass. His reflection might not be as worthy of imitation as he would like it to be." With that piece of wisdom spoken, I yawned and fell asleep.

CHAPTER 3

Porcupine Pete, Quills and Rush

THE LAST DAY

Rush and I were sitting around the dog trailer, eating donuts for lunch. Our people felt that donuts gave hunting dogs more energy when they were in the field. Personally, I feel they like donuts as much as we do. That's okay with me.

As I was thinking about how many quails I had retrieved so far, Rush barked, "Pa, why is this the last day of quail-hunting season?"

I swallowed the final delicious bite of a sugar-coated donut. Scratching my ear (which gave me time to think), I replied, "Ummm, well, Son, quail need time to rest, grow, and replenish their numbers."

Rush blinked twice. "Oh, I... I see. Since this *is* the last day, I'm going to sneak away and explore the bluff above the river bottom. I saw something brown and furry on top of the bluff while hunting yesterday."

"Oh, no. Don't you do that. The people need us to hunt quail. Besides, it could be dangerous. You don't know what you saw. If something happens, we might not be around to help."

BUD-MAN

Lately Rush's personality was more like his great-great-great-granddaddy's, the famous field trial champion dog Esser's Chicoree Hickory Doc better known as Bud-Man. When Bud-Man was young, he was wild, foolish, and stubborn. He would go on adventures in the field. His people would really get upset. Finally, his adventures got him in trouble. Bud-Man never talked about what happened, but he changed. He became a different hunting dog—obedient and responsible. Bud-Man began winning at all the field trial competitions. Then one day a Japanese man rode up on a horse. He said, "I would like to buy Bud-Man for $20,000 and take him to Japan." That was it. Bud-Man headed for Japan.

We were able to buy lots of chow and rawhide chews. We even remodeled our dog houses. Bud-Man would have wanted us to.

Years later Bud-Man came home. He told us how he loved learning about dogs and quail in Japan. But the truth was that he missed his family. Bud-Man always said, "Family is everything."

Rush nudged me. "Pa, Pa, did you hear what I just said?"

"I was thinking about Bud-Man. What did you say?"

"Our hunter won't even know I'm gone. I'll be careful. I know how to take care of myself. I'm practically a grown dog! Besides, I love adventures! This will be fun. Nothing will happen. Honest, Pa." Rush trotted toward the cottonwoods.

"No, you don't, young pup! I put my paw down. I forbid you to go. The people need us."

"But, Pa," he said but then continued, "All right. I'll hunt with you just like I always do."

I wasn't totally convinced Rush was going to obey me. Rush reminded me of his ma, Sly, in several ways. No one could change her mind when she decided to do something. She was very determined. He even looked like her—a total white body with large brown spots. I wondered how I would hunt and keep a watchful eye on him.

PORCUPINE PETE

Later our hunter appeared. It was time to hunt some more. We usually hunted in the morning and late afternoon. We did this until the people got their *limit*. They can only bring home so many quail a day. That way the quail had a chance to replenish.

This season I've been hunting with my son, Rush, so he can learn from me. Our job is to hunt quail, pheasant, and grouse. We all went to hunting school for basic training.

The afternoon was sunny and warm. Our hunter used two dogs at a time to hunt. Rush and I started crisscrossing (like windshield wipers) through the fields. I love running through the prairie grass to find the birds. I could do this all day. This is what I was born to do.

Suddenly, my nose smelled them—the sweet smell of quail. I suppose you are wondering exactly what quail smell like from a dog's point of view. Well, I can tell you they smell like no other smell— sort of a cross between chicken nuggets and fries.

I came up to where the covey (group) of quail was hidden. They were deep in the tall grass. This is when our hunting school training really came in. I didn't want those quail to fly away, so I stopped and pointed to the area where the birds were hiding. I kept my body still with my tail stiff. You might ask why we do that. The answer is simple. Since people don't go to hunting school, they can't find the birds unless we show them where they are. I have often wondered why people don't go to hunting school. Some of them are not very good at bringing the birds down. Today was no exception. The people came up, and the quail flushed. They shot at the flying quail and missed just as we heard a loud, shrill, barking sound—ruff, ruff, *ruuuuf!* That yelping and screeching could only come from one dog—Rush. I looked around but didn't see him. Our hunter blew a whistle twice, which meant for Rush to come back. Still no Rush.

My suspicion was Rush had disobeyed me by going toward the river. I became worried, so I started barking and running straight to the bluff above the river bottom.

I was the first to reach the bluff, so I started climbing. I followed the strange muffled sound, a cross between a *grrrr* and a *ruffffff*. I couldn't believe my eyes when I reached the top. There was Rush, but he had a mouth full of porcupine quills—hardened hair like sharp needles. Porcupines have quills all over their body that protect them from dogs like Rush. I studied that in nature class in hunting school.

The porcupine sat and stared at Rush with a big smile on his face. Rush looked pitiful with quills in his mouth, head, and body. He couldn't even bark properly with those quills sticking out of his mouth.

"Are you his friend?" the porcupine asked me while bending over and licking his belly. The belly of a porcupine does not have quills.

"I'm his pa, and I'm not happy with him. He was supposed to be hunting quail with me. Instead he wandered away to have an *adventure*. Now I find him with quills in his mouth. Dear me, our hunter is not going to be happy. Not at all. This day was supposed to end as a perfect day with lots of quail. Not like this!" I answered in an upset voice.

"I'm not happy either! Your pup has taken hundreds of *my* quills in his mouth. I need those quills. I don't want to wait for the new ones to grow out. Whoever heard of a porcupine without his quills! Just how do you plan to get them back for me, Mr. Hunting Dog?"

Glancing at both Rush and the porcupine, I replied, "Our hunter will take them out at the trailer. Exactly what happened? By the way, my name is Doc, and his is Rush."

"I am Pete. Well, I was minding my own business, having my afternoon snack of bark and twigs. Suddenly, I heard your young pup try to sneak up on me. He actually *pointed* me exactly like your breed does when they find quail. Do I look like a quail? I think not! Anyway, I was so startled that I dropped my bark and twigs. Your young pup proceeded to grab me by the tail with his mouth. Well then, we all know what happened next. He got a mouth full of quills, and I have a bare spot on my tail! Your pup was so stubborn he tried it again and got more quills. He doesn't seem to be very bright." With that lengthy explanation completed, Pete sighed and started licking the bare spot on his tail.

I softly whispered to Pete, "You'd better leave now. The people are here. You can follow us back to our camp and retrieve your quills after our people remove them."

THE MOUTH OF QUILLS

I nudged Rush forward, and we followed our hunter. It was a long walk back for my son. He looked dejected and spent most of the time whimpering with his tail and head down.

By the time we got back to the trailer, the news was all over the woods. Pete told the birds. The birds told the rabbits. The rabbits told the deer. Well, you get the picture.

Patch and Zeke were huddled together by the cottonwood trees when we appeared. They had hunted earlier in the day. Patch, Rush's sister, started howling. She thought Rush looked pretty funny with his mouth wide open and full of quills.

Zeke simply glared at me. He barked, "Well, Doc, I told you so. You spoil the pups, and see what happens. They don't pay any attention to what you tell them to do! I've worked so hard today, and I'm hungry. It will be *hours* before we get home and have chow!"

I was irritated with my brother, and I was definitely tired after all my running in the field. "Zeke, what work did you do? You always pace yourself by walking with our hunter. Then you snatch the birds from the rest of us so it looks like you retrieved them. And the whole time we are the ones that are doing the work!" Zeke knew I was right. He stopped whining.

We all watched while the people pulled each quill from Rush's mouth with needle-nose pliers. It took *two* long hours to get all of the quills out from Rush's mouth and body. Patch, always the inquisitive dog, told me later that she counted the quills. Rush had around a hundred quills in his mouth and more than fifty on the rest of his body.

We then loaded up for the long trip back to the Lazy Dog Hacienda. As we pulled out of the field, I saw Pete and his porcupine friends gathering up the quills. I figured it would take Pete and his friends a long time to get those quills back in Pete.

HOME AND FAMILY

We were all dog-tired when we got home to our kennels, but not too tired to eat the extra dog chow that was waiting for us. Just as I yawned and started to fall asleep, I heard Rush. His voice sounded squeaky. "Pa, I've learned an important thing today."

"Well, Son, what is it?" I knew sleep would have to wait.

"Remember when you said Bud-Man came back

to his kennel because he missed his family?" Rush sat up and peered at me.

"Yep, I remember that story. I'm surprised you were listening, Son." My eyes were getting heavier, and it was hard to keep them open.

"Well, Pa, when I was struggling with Pete and those quills were in my mouth, I got scared. I wished I hadn't taken that adventure! I started worrying that you wouldn't find me and that I would be stuck in the woods with all those quills in my mouth forever! I started missing you—my family."

I sat up. "You know, Son, I think your adventure was a learning experience."

"How did you know that I might get into trouble?" Rush asked with a quizzical look on his face.

I decided to let my son know the age-old secret all hunting dogs keep. Speaking slowly, I said, "Ummm, I guess I need to make a confession, Son. Years ago when I was your age, I decided to disappear when I was on a hunting trip. I found a porcupine in the morning and ended up with quills in my mouth. I was so stubborn I decided to try again in the afternoon. I found another porcupine, and this time I ended up with quills in my shoulder. Never, never again did I disappear for a private adventure on a hunting trip."

"You know, Pa, you're the best," Rush said as he snuggled closer to me.

"So are you, Son," I said as I gently started licking his face.

CHAPTER 4

Hamburgers, Fries, Caesar Salad, and Temptation

HUNGER AND TEMPTATION

Darkness and silence everywhere. Then I heard sounds—shrill and loud. Maybe train whistles or boat fog horns?

My body jerked. I blinked, stood up, shook myself off, and realized it was night. The sounds were only Zeke's snoring! Of all the dog runs at the Lazy Dog Hacienda, why was I next to him? Usually, I slept inside because I was the oldest and wisest. So why was I outside? Oh, yes, now I remember—*hunger and temptation!*

It all started earlier this evening. Snoozing in my comfortable brown chair in the house, I was aroused by the sounds of strange people noises. Thinking they came to play with me, I quickly trotted through the house, stopping to sniff people's legs. The people expected it, and they were quite disappointed if you didn't. As you sniff, they reach down, pat you on the head, and step away. It's a good way to get attention and a *pat* or two. I think it's a form of *hello* for them—but for me it's a way to find out whether they have dogs. As Zeke, my brother, says, "Why waste our time on people who don't have dogs?"

After making my rounds through the people, I noticed that one in particular was staring at me. I pay attention to that one because he took me hunting. We knew him as one of our people. He was the hunter, the great one. It was obvious he wanted me to leave. You could tell by the fact that his eyes started to glaze over with that certain *stare*. I quickly trotted into the chow room, better known as the dining room.

Instantly, my nose got a whiff of hamburgers and fries. What a temptation! All those warm hamburgers and fries covered with foil sitting on the dining room table. And the people were busy talking and would not even notice that I was in the chow room.

Personally, a dog of my stature liked more than warm hamburgers and fries, but in a pinch they'll do. *The foil is a nice touch*, I thought to myself. I put my front paws on the table, used my long nose and mouth to lift the foil up, and then I gobbled down *all* of the hamburgers and fries. Then I pushed the foil down so the crime scene was clean.

A DOG'S DELIGHT

Suddenly, I smelled *it*! I hopped down and with a burst of energy, and I ran into the kitchen. There it was, sitting on the edge of the blue tile countertop. I had had dreams about it—Caesar salad laced with anchovies (small salty fish) covered with thick oil dressing plus croutons and cheese. In our world we called it "a dog's delight." And to top it off, they put it in a large round bowl just like my food bowl outside.

Yep, another temptation! But Caesar salad was my all-time favorite. The people *were* in the other room. I thought, *If they were really hungry, they would be chowing down right now. I bet they really wanted me to have it.* My stomach growled, making it harder to resist eating the salad.

I inched up to the white cabinet doors. I stood on my two back legs, placed my paws on either side of the bowl, and gobbled the salad down.

Smacking my lips, I finished the last morsel from the sides of the bowl. As I flopped down, my paws accidently pushed the bowl onto the orange tile floor. It sounded like a baseball bat hitting the floor. *Boom, boom, bang!* It made such a racket that people started swarming into the kitchen, including the great one. He was leading the charge and did not seem pleased with what had happened. No more pats on the head for me. His face turned red just like that tomato juice the people had put on me right after I'd been skunked. He had a crazed look in his eyes as he lunged for me. So what's a dog to do? I slipped out the back door into the garage. Our hunter proceeded to follow me, which was really a bad choice on his part. He tripped on a skateboard, which sent him sailing through the back door, and he landed in the garage on the concrete floor. For a minute he looked like a turtle flying through the air. His legs and arms straight out, while his tummy seemed attached to the skateboard. I never knew people could fly like that.

THE CHASE

By the time the great one landed, I was already out of the garage and into the pasture. He started chasing me around the pasture and hollering something about "the wrecked dinner." It's hard to understand people. The "wrecked dinner" was in my stomach! It was the best chow I'd had in a long time. Didn't our hunter know that I'd actually saved him from having to hunt for our dinner?

Pretty soon, I began to feel poorly. I think I ate one too many anchovies. I decided it was time to let the great one catch up, figuring he would be pleased that I had licked my bowl clean. He wasn't. I ended up sleeping in the dog run instead of on my warm, comfortable brown chair, which brings me back to my situation with my brother and his snoring.

ZEKE'S ANSWER

Zeke let out another loud snore. Annoyed, I clenched my teeth and barked, "Zeke, stop snoring."

Zeke moaned. "Ummm, what about my snoring? You're just mad because your hunger and temptation caused you to end up sleeping out here with us! You let your weakness for people chow get the best of you."

I stretched my body and scratched my ear before answering. I needed to reflect on what Zeke just said. *Is it possible that I, Doc, the oldest and wisest dog, had actually let chow tempt me into doing wrong? Will I need to concede that for once that selfish, "everything my way" Zeke is right?*

Stunned, I barked, "Zeke, for once you are right. I had no self-control when it came to Caesar salad, hamburgers, and fries. I was tempted by the chow, and I gave in to my temptation."

Zeke nodded, sat up straight, and puffed his chest

out to look noble. "Of course, I'm right. After all, I am the smartest dog in the bunch. Now where was I? Oh, yes, as I was saying, you know I snore because I have a *special* nose. The hump in my nose gives me extra room for collecting smells—bird, skunk, porcupine, people, and all kinds. My special nose was passed down from our ancestors. Didn't I tell you about it?"

"Yes, you've told me many times." Then it occurred to me that when Zeke talked, he wasn't snoring. "You know, Zeke, I would love to hear your story again."

Zeke eyed me suspiciously, paused, and then continued, "As I was about to say ..."

Finally, I realized what was happening. My real punishment for giving in to temptation was not being out in the dog run but having to listen to Zeke tell the same stories over and over again!

CHAPTER 5

Zeke and the Cabbage Patch Skunk

BIRTHDAYS AND EIGHT-DOG TRAILERS

My birthday that fateful January started out like any other hunting day. But before the day was over, adventure would strike the Hickory family once again!

Our hunter, the great one, was up before the sun. That could mean only one thing. We were going hunting! I can always tell because my nose gets a whiff of that delightful aroma of all kinds of manure, grass, leaves, and other unmentionables as he tracks through the house wearing those old brown hunting boots. Our hunter puts on the canvas pants and shirt. They usually have parts of bird feathers still stuck on them. Sometimes those tufts of bird feathers will stay on him for a while before they drop off, almost as if the quail were leaving their calling cards. I figure that shows not only where the great one and I have been but also what great hunters we are.

"Doc, Zeke, get the others up. We are going hunting," our hunter shouted.

Yawning and stretching, I pulled myself out of a deep sleep. I was just dreaming of chasing and finding birds. We got the other dogs up. The people started loading our eight-dog trailer. This was what the eight of us had trained for—the hunting fields and birds!

As I started to jump up into the trailer, Zeke pushed me down and hopped up first. He always had the impression our ancestors were the *blue bloods* of Germany, which entitled him to be *first* in every situation. I had no patience for this since I was lying flat on my back on the cold gray driveway.

"Zeke, stop pushing in front of everyone. Don't you know that is very rude?" I struggled to turn over and get back up again. I have very long legs like a camel, so it takes me a little longer to get up most of the time. I was considered a rather large German shorthaired pointer.

My brother sat up inside the trailer, trying to look regal with his chest puffed out. Zeke snarled, looked at me, and said, "The nobles are always first!"

Yeah, right. How I wish Zeke would stop trying to be so self-important and selfish. I've always thought since he was ticked that he was jealous of my solid liver color. I have always felt that the ticked-colored German shorthaired pointers are basically crazy. Zeke proves that daily.

I was almost in the trailer when I noticed Zeke squinting his eyes and looking at a half-eaten rawhide on the ground. He jumped on and over me, once again pushing me down. There I was again, feet in the air, staring at the sky.

I was beginning to get a little upset at my brother, so I barked, "Zeke, *please* watch what you are doing."

Zeke grabbed the rawhide. "Doc, you know perfectly well that I need a snack in the morning to get started. It's not my fault you were in the way. Our great-grandfather Baron Von Dar Windstorm *always* ate before the royalty took him hunting."

I growled as I struggled to jump into the trailer. "I'm sick and tired of hearing about our Baron Von ..." Zeke held the rawhide in his mouth and used my body as a ladder. He jumped back into the trailer while pushing me down. This time I saw stars in the sky as I landed with my back on the driveway. Then our people came around and put each of us in our trailer stalls.

THE FIRST BLINK

As we settled in the trailer, Zeke and I gave each other *the stare*. This consisted of looking directly at each other without blinking. Zeke usually got impatient and started whining or bragging. This caused him to break eye contact. Just as we started for parts unknown to us, Zeke blinked first. He complained, "I don't know why our people put me back here in the trailer. I deserve to be up in the truck with them because I have a royal bloodline. Our great-grandfather Baron Von Dar Windstorm would never have ridden in a *dog* trailer. Hey, there is not enough hay in here. You have more hay in your stall than I do. That's not fair. Honestly—"

Annoyed, I spoke up, "Zeke, I'm not interested in our ancestors. They didn't have dog trailers back then. You have as much hay in your stall as I do. Please stop chattering so we can get some sleep before our big hunt. Remember, you like to get plenty of rest before you hunt." That usually shut Zeke up. The only thing he liked better than gabbing was sleeping.

I noticed the scenery changing as we rode through western Oklahoma. We saw fewer houses and more woods and fields of grass. We went off the highway into the woods and through pastures filled with shinnery. Shinnery is a people word for stunted scrub oak. Finally, we reached our destination. Our people pulled up near a creek surrounded by cottonwood and walnut trees. They would hunt with two of us at a time so that we didn't get too tired. The let Zeke and me out of the trailer, but guess who leaped out first? Naturally, it was Zeke.

Trembling with excitement, I could feel the cold air. It was perfect weather for hunting and running after those birds!

Zeke rolled his eyes and said, "Oh, here we are again. I'm going to have to act like I am *so* interested in this. Doc, I get first dibs on walking with the hunter. There is no point in running all around and wearing myself down. My bloodline is known for pacing itself."

I wanted to say that my brother's weird part of the bloodline was also known for whining, bragging, and being selfish. Instead I just nodded and let Zeke push in front. The day was young, and there was time to straighten Zeke out.

HUNTING SCHOOL

We are taught a great deal about quail in hunting school. I received an A+ in quail class. Quail sleep in little coveys (groups) hidden where hunters can't find them. We can find them because of our keen smell. They have a distinct smell similar to a freshly baked pie—sweet apple pie.

As soon as the quail smell becomes strong, we stop and put our tails up. People call that "being on point." Then we wait until our hunters catch up with us, so the birds will flush (fly), and the hunters will shoot the quail. Actually, hunters are *supposed* to shoot them, but sometimes they aren't very good at that part. That is when it can be frustrating. You knock yourself out in hunting school, working like a dog to bring home the good grades. Eagerly, you get up early and travel hours to the hunting fields. Then by covering miles of territory, you find and point the quail. Patiently, you stay on point while waiting for the people to catch up, and then they miss the shot! You can be the best bird dog in the world, but if the hunters are lousy shots, you have just wasted your talent. Zeke really complains when this happens!

Now where was I in this story? Oh, yes, now I remember. Zeke and I started hunted the land in front of us, crisscrossing back and forth like tying shoelaces. Zeke was supposed to be running like me, but of course, he was walking with our hunter.

Suddenly, Zeke came up to me and barked, "I'm only walking with our people so I can save myself for the harder part of hunting later on."

Tired and irritated, I said, "No, you are walking close to the great one until all the work is completed. We hunt, find, point, flush, and start to retrieve. Then you jump in and grab the birds to take back and impress the people." Zeke glared at me and then went back with our people.

FAMILIAR SMELL

After crisscrossing for an hour, I recognized the sweet and sour smell of something familiar. What could that smell be? It smelled like sour milk, blue cheese dressing, or very old bacon. I turned to ask Zeke, but he was far behind with our people.

I started barking and running faster. I could hear our people yelling something in the background. Then I heard Zeke barking, but I kept running up and down the hills until I got to thick brush. I stopped dead in my tracks. That horrible smell became stronger. It definitely was not sour milk, old bacon, or blue cheese dressing. But what was it?

Just then I saw something running through the brush toward what the people called a wild cabbage patch. The animal was traveling too fast for me to recognize it. I knew it wasn't quail. But I was trained to find and bring back game. I was never told it could only be birds. So what's a German shorthaired pointer to do, right? I ran straight for it.

However, the smell of that animal became stronger and more unpleasant the closer I got. It began to remind me of what the people, especially the other one, claimed she loved to eat. They always seemed to have some left to put in our chow. She claimed we needed healthy people food mixed with our dog food. I knew better than that. They just gave us scrapes of their food that they didn't want! Why didn't they give us their hamburgers? After all, that is real healthy food, especially for dogs. Probably by now you've figured out that smell. It was the smell of cooked *sauerkraut*!

Zeke, sensing I was getting close to some type

of game, came running toward me. This would be a dead run for him but a fast trot for me. He shrieked, "Doc, stop. I *must* be first. I'm the leader, you know. After all my work today, I deserve to find the special game for the great one."

I started to say something, but then I saw the black and white bushy-tailed animal. Suddenly, I remembered what it was, and it was not a pleasant memory! I stopped dead in my tracks, pointed, and waited for Zeke to catch up. As he approached, I barked, "You know, Zeke, you are right. Please feel free to go in front of me. Our hunter will be very proud of your special game animal."

THE CABBAGE PATCH SKUNK

Before I could step aside, Zeke, who was as selfish as ever, leaped over me and right into the black and white animal. He looked shocked and pale even for a ticked liver and white dog. The animal lifted its tail and started spraying Zeke with a foul odor—much worse than cooked sauerkraut or even broccoli!

Zeke was furious he had been sprayed, and

realizing that he had collided with a skunk, he began tossing the animal high over the cabbage patch. Startled, it tried to spray him again. This was quite a sight to see! The animal kept spraying, and Zeke kept tossing. Cabbages were flying everywhere. I got closer and saw Zeke's eyes. He began to squint. Tears were rolling down from his eyes because of the fumes, but he was *mad* and wouldn't quit tossing and growling. Finally, the skunk got away and made one last leap over the cabbages and through the nice red rosebushes with thorns.

I chased them both, but from a distance. I heard a shriek, howl, and then growling. Then I saw what appeared to be Zeke. Cabbage leaves and thorns all over him. Zeke was on the ground, and the skunk was nowhere to be found. What impressed me about Zeke was that he had a red rose hanging from his mouth. My brother had time to pick a red rose from the bush even after all that. I started howling. Zeke had his tail down and started running back to our hunter!

Yes, indeed, I do believe it was the same skunk that sprayed me last year!

THE RED SHORTHAIR

It was quite embarrassing for Zeke. Our hunter was not happy about Zeke's special game animal. Zeke's head and tail were down. He was humiliated and ashamed. No dog likes being skunked, especially a dog that thinks he is royalty. The smell was horrible! And to top it off, Zeke almost turned red from all the tomato juice the great one put on him just to get rid of the smell.

My brother sheepishly turned to me while he was airing out in the dog run that evening. "Doc, I think I'll be more patient next time and let you go first."

I barked, "Zeke, that is quite all right. You can go first any time you wish. Maybe this will help you realize that you do not always stay ahead or get what you want by jumping in front of someone else."

Zeke nodded his head in agreement. You know, I am pretty smart when it comes to dealing with Zeke.

CHAPTER 6

Willie's First Secret

STOLEN FOOD

"Who stole my food?" Zeke growled. He pawed at his empty food bowl. Then he started pacing back and forth while eyeing my food. "Doc, you still have some."

I gobbled the rest of my food down before I barked. "Hmmm, I noticed yesterday some of my food was gone when we returned. The pups didn't take it. They're at hunting school this week." I sat down next to my empty bowl and scratched my ear. What a mystery—the disappearance of our food!

Zeke's body quivered, and his eyes went from

the size of baseballs to tiny slits. "Honestly, Doc, don't you get upset about anything? This is *very* important. Some dog took our food! I need to keep my strength up while working around here. Look at the enormous energy I use chasing birds every morning."

"What work? Chasing birds is not work. It's fun. I haven't noticed you working. You *usually* eat and snooze."

"You ask what work?" Zeke snarled. "Well, for one, taking care of the pups."

I grinned and muttered, "That will be the day."

THE COMMOTION

There was a commotion by the swing set. I heard the sound of a bird calling *jay-jay, jay-jay*. I looked up and saw Willie, Patch's crow friend, flying close to the ground. The other bird chased Willie around the pine trees and through the playhouse. I heard Willie squeal. "My black feathers are special."

The other bird shouted, "Well, *my* feathers are beautiful colors—blue, white, and gray."

Nature class taught us the names of birds by their sounds and colors. The other bird was a blue jay.

"Doc, are you listening to me?" Zeke said. He quit pacing, sat down, and puffed his chest out. "Every time I explain something to you, I have the feeling you're not paying attention!"

My brain is muddled enough without listening to everything Zeke says. I didn't want to argue, so I answered, "That's not true. I'm thinking. Why is Willie playing with a Blue Jay? Crows and blue jays don't play with one another. Remember, Zeke, in nature class when we learned blue jays were known for taking and hoarding other birds' food."

"Yes, but maybe Willie needed another bird to play with since Patch is gone. Besides, that's not *our* problem. We need to solve the mystery of our missing food." Impatient, Zeke started pacing back and forth again.

"I guess so." I scratched my ear one more time for good measure. It always helped me think. "Hey, Zeke, I have an idea. Tomorrow morning we can leave just a few morsels in our food bowls. Then we can go on our morning rounds of the pasture like we always do before coming back and hiding by the swing set to see what happens to our food."

Zeke sat back on his haunches. "Doc, I hate leaving my food bowl without cleaning it completely with my tongue, but in the interest of solving this mystery, I *suppose* it's all right."

THE SURPRISE

We were up bright and early the next morning. The people gave us our food. Zeke grumbled, "They always give you more."

"No, they don't." I stared at Zeke until he broke the stare by munching his food. It always worked. Zeke couldn't stand to keep staring, especially with food around.

We left morsels of food in our bowls and started on our morning rounds so we wouldn't arouse suspicion.

The prairie grass is taller than us, so tall in fact that we lost track of each other. I chased a few birds before barking, "Zeke, Zeke, we need to go back." There was silence. Maybe he didn't hear me. Once again I barked, "Zeke, Zeke." Silence. I raised my head up and heard a strange sound. It came from an area covered with grass and trees. It sounded like a can of seeds being shaken. It reminded me of those horrible things the people babies held—baby rattles. I remembered times when I slept peacefully until the human baby crawled up and banged my nose with a rattle. Surely, a baby wasn't in the pasture. My body shuttered just thinking about it. I ran toward the sound.

Zeke's body was rigid when I ran up, stumbled, and smashed into him. He blended in with the prairie grass. His speckled liver and white coat mixed in with the yellow, green, and tan of the grass. Zeke lost his balance and fell on a grayish, white, and black rattlesnake in our pasture. The snake coiled and vibrated its tail, which made the rattle sound. It struck at Zeke. Terrified, Zeke yelped and bounced higher than a basketball.

The snake looked puzzled, choked, and then spit something out. "Ugh! You taste like old, worn shoe leather. This isn't my day. Of all the dogs in the neighborhood, why did I pick you to strike?" The snake shook his body and slithered off.

"Ouch, that hurt! I can't believe you ran into me, Doc."

"I am sorry, Zeke, but it's hard to see in this grass."

Zeke began licking the spot where the snake struck him. "Did you notice how well I handled the snake?"

"Not really. It looked like the rattlesnake simply spit you out. I take it you don't taste very good, at least not to snakes." I was astonished that Zeke actually thought he had handled the snake and not the other way around!

VILLAINS

Zeke muttered as we crept to the swing set, "After all we've been through this morning, we'd better catch the villain that's stealing our food."

"Let's hide behind the sandbox," I whispered. "The railroad ties around the sandbox will give us great cover. It's a perfect place to hide!"

We crouched down with only our eyes and ears peering from behind the sandbox. Pretty soon, we saw Willie fly up to our food bowls. He landed on Zeke's bowl and looked around. First, he ate some food. Then he grabbed pieces of food in his beak, flew over the swimming pool, and landed by an oak tree. Willie put the food down. He hopped to a leaf, dragged it to the food, and carefully placed it on top. We watched while he did this several more times. After stopping to rest, Willie flew off.

I was bewildered. It wasn't a *dog* stealing our food. It was *Willie.*

"Aha, just as I thought," Zeke said. "You befriend a crow, and look what happens. What are we going to do? How will we get our food back? I want Willie stopped!"

"Hush, Zeke. Be patient. I need to figure this out. I didn't plan on it being Willie. First, we need to find out why Willie is taking our food. Then—"

Before I said anymore, we heard *"Jay-jay, jay-jay."* The blue jay flew down, lifted the leaf up, and snatched the food, and then off he went.

"Doc, look. The blue jay is stealing the food that Willie stole from us. I can't believe it! *Our* food is going everywhere. Oh, my, this is *terrible.*"

"You're right, Zeke, but we need to follow the trail of food to find the answers to our mystery."

We chased after the blue jay. He went around to the front yard and stopped at the walnut tree. He dropped *our* food in his nest. We followed him back to Willie's oak tree. He picked up more food and then went around to the front yard and dropped it in his nest again.

In the meantime, Willie went back to our dog runs. He grabbed food and placed it under a leaf near his oak tree. He was so busy flying back and forth that he didn't even notice the blue jay or the fact that his food was gone.

"Doc, I'm getting dizzy." Zeke groaned after going from oak to walnut tree and back again. "We've been doing this all day. We need to get our food back, but I'm dog-tired."

My legs were weak from running all day. I began to wobble. I plopped myself down on the grass. Fortunately, we were by our doghouses. "Zeke, you're right. We need to confront Willie and the blue jay, but the doghouses *do* look inviting. Let's sleep on this. We can catch Willie in the act tomorrow."

A DILEMMA

The next morning we were gobbling our food when Willie flew over us. He landed, stood erect, and with his two stick legs, marched toward us like the leader in a school band.

"Zeke, Doc, we need to talk." The closer he got, the lower his head went. Willie was glum. "I, I have a *dilemma.*"

I barked, "You don't say."

Zeke snarled and showed his teeth, although they were basically only nubs now since his favorite pastime was chewing on our chain-link dog runs. There was no doubt about it. They sure were nubs. But Zeke's nubs did sparkle like silver when the sun was bright.

"Patience, Zeke," I muttered. "Willie, you know we're your friends. We're here to help you. What is your dilemma?"

"Yes, well, I have a confession to make." Willie gasped and then continued, "I decided to take your food to store away for winter instead of finding my own. You had so much, and I didn't think you would miss it."

Zeke bellowed, "Not miss it! Of course we missed it. I'm sure I've lost weight since you've taken our food. It's hard enough to guard our food against other dogs at the Lazy Dog Hacienda without having to worry about guarding it against crows. We want it back. Every last morsel!"

"Well, that's just it. It's all gone. That's my dilemma. The blue jay stole it from me. I followed the blue jay back to his nest, where all my food—actually, your food—was. I made a mistake. It's like a complete circle of wrongs. Now I know how it feels to have your food stolen. I promise I won't steal anymore of your dog food! How can we stop the blue jay from taking our food? I mean, *your food.*" Willie hung his head even lower. He approached me and stood on the top edge of my water bowl.

"Aha. I've got it!" I sprang to my paws, knocking poor Willie into the water. He flapped his wings, coughed, and flew out.

"Hey, what do you have, Doc?" Zeke asked excitedly.

"Yes, what do you have?" Willie asked as he landed to the right of my water bowl.

MYSTERY SOLVED

"The blue jay can't take our food if there isn't any," I barked with authority.

"What, what do you mean?" Zeke said, stuttering. "I want our food back."

"Look, the blue jay already has our food. We can't get that particular food back, but we can stop him from taking more. Willie, didn't you say you were sorry?" I barked.

Willie nodded yes and flapped his wings.

"Didn't you also say you weren't going to steal anymore?" I stared directly at Willie's eyes.

"Yes, I learned my lesson," Willie cawed.

I sat straight up, glanced at both Zeke and Willie, and said, "Well, that's it! We'll make sure we finish our food in the morning. No food, no blue jay. He'll move on to a new neighborhood."

From that time onward, Zeke and I licked our bowls clean in the morning. Willie found food for the winter and stored it in a place the blue jay didn't find. The blue jay tired of not being able to take our food, so he moved on to another neighborhood. The mystery of our stolen food was solved. However, Willie had two more secrets we would soon learn, but that's for another time.

CHAPTER 7

Sly and the Boys: Catch of the Day, Part 1

DONUTS, SLY, AND PUPPY LOVE

Have you ever heard the song, "Let me tell you about the birds and the bees and the thing called puppy love"? Well, Zeke or I hadn't either.

Long ago on a warm September morning, Zeke and I were hunting. By noon it was hot. Our people decided it was time to walk back to the trailer and have lunch. On the way, Zeke started whining about his paws hurting. "Doc, I'm soooo tired. I hope our people appreciate how hard I worked to find those birds for them. My pads are sore, and I'm thirsty and hungry. What do you think they brought us for lunch? Probably those day-old donuts *they* think we love so much. Are we almost there? Why did we park so far away from where we hunt?"

"Zeke, you aren't the only one finding birds for our people. Give a little credit to me. I'm hot and tired today, but you don't hear me complaining about it!"

We finally arrived at the trailer. Another hunter and his dog would join us for the afternoon hunt. The hunter drove up as we were munching our donuts. I remember it like it was yesterday. She jumped gracefully from his truck as if in slow motion. You could see the beauty of her sleek muscled body. She had a snow-white coat with a touch of liver (brown) on her back and tail. Her eyes were a soft brown, and they were set deep between her slender nose. I was in love.

The hunter called her Sly. Her official name was Rawhide's Sly. Her pedigree was the envy of all who knew her, including Zeke. Her father was the famous Rawhide's Clown. He won the German Shorthaired Pointer Club of America's All-Age National Championship for three consecutive years. Oakridge's Silver Bullet was her mother's name, a champion in her own right.

BROTHERLY LOVE?

I looked at Zeke and noticed his eyes were pointed straight at Sly.

His body quivered with excitement, which surprised me. There were times he quivered when mad or scared but never when meeting a new dog—until now.

"Zeke, isn't she beautiful? I'm in love," I exclaimed with a soft voice.

Zeke eyed me with a suspicious look. "Doc, don't be silly. I saw her first. You saw the way her eyes met mine. Even your small brain can see she looked adoringly at me!"

Before I had time to answer, Sly came over and joined us. Zeke puffed his chest out and barked.

"Sly, I'm the best hunting dog our people have.

My sense of smell is great for finding quail. In hunting school I made straight A's. The hunters thought I had the most promise. Why, our great-grandfather Baron Von Dar Windstorm was a champion hunting dog. He hunted with the royalty of Germany."

This went on and on. Finally, I had enough of hearing about Zeke. As I opened my mouth to speak, our people yelled, "Doc, Zeke, Sly, it's time to go back in the field. The quail should be in the north part of the Packsaddle Ranch."

WINDSHIELD WIPERS

I knew Zeke would show off for Sly the moment we went in the field. When we started hunting, we crisscrossed back and forth like windshield wipers through the grass and trees. Suddenly, Zeke disappeared. Sly looked up and said, "Doc, where did Zeke go? He's too fast for me."

I didn't believe what I was hearing. Zeke moving fast? What a joke. Zeke didn't move fast. My brother liked to stay behind close to our hunter—Zeke calls it "pacing himself"— I call it a slow creep. While

Zeke is with our people, I'm usually knocking myself out, finding and pointing a covey (group) of quail. When I get on point, the hunters come up, flush the birds, and bring some down. Zeke, of course, will stop (honor the point) when I go on point. But just as soon as a bird is down and I start to retrieve it, Zeke dashes past me, grabs the bird, and brings it back to our hunter. Zeke loves doing this because he gets all the pats on the head for retrieving the bird.

CATCH OF THE DAY

I debated whether or not I should tell Sly the truth. Zeke was just trying to show off for her. I barked, "You know, Sly, why don't you stay here and wait for the hunters. I'll go find Zeke." My little brother wasn't going to get the best of me! I knew what he was doing. Zeke was trying to find special game to bring back and show off for Sly! My brother wasn't the only one who could find special game.

I started running through the bushes, tall grasses, and trees. Finally, I came to a dry creek bed, but the soil was still moist. Did I smelled something rather different? I stopped and looked down, and I saw there was an underground tunnel. The opening was larger than a gopher's hole, but the smell was coming from there. It smelled like sour milk—kind of a sweet but sour smell! Of course, it was a den for some weird animal. We learned about all types of smells and game in hunting school. I knew I had to have it! I started digging with my front paws as fast as possible. Sand and dirt were flying all around me. Dust whirled in the air like a tornado. Finally, my paws hit something very hard. What was a dog to do? I knew in my heart of hearts I should stop, but the thought of Zeke bringing the best catch of the day to show off to Sly simply made me angry. The smell seemed to get stronger. Finally, I had enough of the hard area exposed so that I could grab what looked like a very strange and long animal. I have a very large head, and I can open my mouth wide, so I was able to pull the animal from its den. I pulled, but it resisted. Eventually, the animal and I were one! I ended up sitting back on my haunches with the odd-smelling animal in my mouth. Again, what was a dog to do? If I had let go of the animal, I would have lost the battle. I had to bring the animal back to Sly and show her that I was the best hunting dog of all, much better than show-off Zeke!

The animal struggled to get away from my jaw, but to no avail. It was brown-colored, and its body was covered with a leathery, armor-like skin. It had a pointed snout that reminded me of Zeke's long nose. The paws seemed to have sharp claws. Fortunately, the legs were short, so the claws could not reach me. I knew I had to get back to Sly and our people to show them my catch of the day.

By the time I made it back, my jaws were sore from carrying this strange looking animal. Sly was sitting next to my hunter. I lifted my head high in a rather regal way, puffed my chest out, and held the animal directly in front of my hunter. We are taught in hunting school that when we bring birds back, we hold them in our mouth until our hunters take them from us. Of course, I *knew* this wasn't a quail bird, but I still held it in my mouth. The look on my hunter's face was one of shock. Sly started backing away. Where was the praise from my hunter and Sly?

My hunter looked at me and shouted, "Doc,

you are supposed to be bringing back quail, not armadillos!"

I couldn't believe what I was hearing. My hunter didn't want my find. After all my traveling over hills and through woods just to bring this huge, hard-shelled animal back in my mouth, and I don't get any respect from my hunter for my catch of the day. Unbelievable. Perhaps I just didn't hear him correctly.

"Doc," my hunter said, "quit prancing around Sly and me, trying to show off with that animal. Get rid of it right now!"

Then I endured the most embarrassing thing that a hunter could do to a wonderful hunting dog like me. He started laughing. Sly started howling. My great catch of the day turned into the worst. How humiliating. All I could think of was how I just wanted to impress Sly and get the better of my brother, Zeke. Surely I was not becoming like Zeke, always trying to impress hunters and other dogs. That wasn't me, right?

Just as I was thinking about my situation, the armadillo started wiggling. I bowed my head in shame and walked off slowly. When I was out of sight from both Sly and my hunter, I dropped the armadillo.

ARMADILLO WISDOM

"Well, it's about time. How dare you grab me from my den and drag me all this way! I was having my lunch of ants and grubs when you just grabbed me. What a day! You are the second *hunting dog* to-day that has tried to drag me from my den! The first one called himself 'Zeke, the Special Game Dog.' Can you imagine that? He tried to talk me out of my den by telling me that he was from royalty. His pedigree papers showed that. Do I look like someone that cares about pedigrees? Then Zeke told me Sly, the hunting dog he wanted to impress, just wanted to see me. What a joke! I would never believe that. All Zeke did was bark, bark, bark, trying to get me out of my den! I guess he didn't want to get his paws dirty trying to grab me from my den. He wasn't as determined as you were. So I convinced him that if he really wanted to impress the dog called Sly, he should go over to the south pasture where the calves were. Now, that's really *big* game. And he actually believed me! By the way, what's your name? My name is Arnie." Having said all that, the armadillo licked a claw and started looking around for another one of his dens. Armadillos were known for having more than one den.

"My name is Doc. But I can't believe what I am hearing. You mean to say that my brother, Zeke, was here before me and now has moved on to finding *calves*? Calves aren't our kind of game. Even I know that."

"You are right, Doc. That's what Zeke was going to do. I couldn't believe it either. I just said that to get rid of him. It was easy. You might want to go after him, though. Those cows are with their young calves, and they get pretty mad when some hunting dog wants to grab a calf."

I started running toward the south pasture where Zeke had gone. Both Zeke and I needed to get back to our hunter and Sly. Our job was hunting quail, not finding any special catches.

As Arnie watched me leave, another armadillo came up. Arnie turned to him and said, "See, Son.

That's how you get rid of those supposedly smart hunting dogs. It may have taken me longer with Doc, but in the end, I used the same idea. Just send them to their next special game. Then Arnie and his son moved on to another den.

CHAPTER 8

Sly and the Boys: Catch of the Day, Part 2

QUAIL OR COWS?

I began to think about what Arnie, the armadillo, and I talked about as I ran through the south pasture trying to find Zeke. Was it possible that my annoying brother had really been fooled by an armadillo? Yes, Zeke could be stubborn and selfish sometimes, but he was rarely fooled by any animal—except, of course, me. I needed to give Arnie credit for how he convinced Zeke to leave him alone and go chase other special game, especially if Zeke was going after calves. I certainly would never let a mere armadillo fool me. Now I was running through the pasture, trying to find my brother before he got into trouble with calves.

I heard a terrible commotion coming from the direction of some scrub oaks and tall grass. Leaves, grass, and sticks were flying everywhere. It sounded like an animal was upset or in pain. I heard a very loud shrill cry of mooeee, mooeee. I crept closer. I spotted Zeke with a baby calf in the tall blue-stem grass. He had his teeth clamped down on the neck of the calf, and he was trying to pull it toward me. I couldn't believe my eyes. I started barking. The calf was bawling while he dug his hooves into the ground. It was hard to figure out who was pulling who. Zeke stopped and released the loose skin of the calf's neck. Then Zeke puffed his chest out, glared at me, and touted, "I wouldn't be barking if I were you, Doc. Let's see you bring this size of game back to Sly and our hunters. They will be soooo proud of me."

I could hear barking in the distance. It could be only one dog—Sly. Zeke and I both started barking. Soon Sly appeared. My brother immediately looked directly at Sly. "See what I found for you. Talk about being a good hunting dog. I'm the best. I can find, catch, and retrieve any game, including this calf." The calf started bawling again just as Zeke finished barking.

I stopped barking because I saw what was behind Zeke. Sly's eyes grew as big as water bowls. We both stepped back.

Zeke looked puzzled. "Why are you backing up? Don't you want to come closer to *my* catch. Our hunters will be surprised when they see this calf."

I said, "You are right about our people being surprised. We are supposed to be hunting birds, not calves! You'd better turn around and—"

"Stop right there, Doc," Zeke said sharply. "You are jealous because I found the biggest game of all. Sly can see what a great hunting dog I am. I found and retrieved a calf!"

Sly barked, "Zeke, watch out!"

THE CIRCLE

The calf gathered its footing and looked directly at Zeke. Then suddenly, it turned around and started running away from Zeke, Sly, and me. Caught off guard, Zeke turned around and started trembling. About ten cows began to surround Zeke. Sly and I backed away. There was almost a complete circle around Zeke composed of big cows and the calf.

Sly's voice sounded scared as she barked. "Zeke, get out of there before the cows completely surround you!" The warning came too late. The circle was complete.

Zeke started howling for help. "Doc, *please* help me." As Zeke barked those words, one cow with the calf next to her pawed the ground and came closer to Zeke. This was the largest of all the cows. She glared at Zeke.

"Zeke," I barked. "That cow is the mother of the calf. She looks angry. You'd better get out of there. Run, little brother." With his head down, Zeke started shaking and trembling. Yes, even his short tail was trembling. Zeke was scared! He was so scared that he couldn't move. His four paws were stuck to the ground like he was caught in wet cement.

What could I do? I couldn't let those cows hurt Sly or even my younger brother. I immediately ran through the circle of cows and stopped next to Zeke. *These cows are huge*, I thought. I was one of the tallest German shorthaired pointers probably in the whole world, and yet I looked small compared to those cows. What a big problem!

Thinking fast, I turned to the mother cow and barked, "Zeke, was trying to show off by bringing your calf to us. He had no intention of hurting it. He merely wanted to show us what a beautiful calf it is. Isn't that right, Zeke?"

In the most pitiful and shrill bark he could muster, Zeke said, "Yes, that's right. *Please, please* let me go!"

The mother cow started to smile. "Girls, let them go. We all know the ticked dog was not very bright when he grabbed my calf. He is much smaller than we are. He can't hurt us. Why, his brother has to get him out of trouble. Look how silly he looks trembling and howling for help. Remember that *we* are much bigger than you. This is our neighborhood. You are not welcome here." After saying that, the mother, the calf, and the rest of the cows strolled away.

We heard whistles in the distance as the cows were leaving. Zeke stopped shaking, lifted his head up, and starting running toward the sound of whistles. He barked, "Let's go, Sly. Come on, Doc. Our hunters are whistling for us to come back." It was strange how Zeke could act like nothing happened when only a few minutes before he was so scared.

Zeke started moving the hay around his stall in the dog trailer on our way back to the Lazy Dog Hacienda. He liked to pile it up so that his bed was softer. Usually, Zeke liked to whine about how the rest of us hunting dogs had more hay than he did, but not today. Those cows must have really upset him. Finally, Zeke barked, "You know, Doc, I was trying to impress Sly by bringing back the a calf, but my plan backfired."

I scratched behind my ear before answering. It amazed me that my little brother would actually understand what had really happened. He almost caused those cows to get so mad they could have hurt us! Maybe Zeke really got it!

Just as I was about to tell Zeke my part of the story about Arnie, the armadillo, my brother barked, "Our great-grandfather Baron Von Dar Windstorm would point and retrieve birds and even track large game they called deer. That's what our German ancestors would do. Honestly, it's our hunter's fault that we couldn't bring back that calf. I haven't had the proper training. Since our ancestors have been in America, all those hunting schools have only taught the German shorthaired pointers how to find and retrieve birds! After all, our breed is really known as an all-game hunting dog, especially in Germany. I need to tell Sly that it certainly wasn't *my* fault that I could not bring back that calf. It was the hunter's fault. He didn't train me properly!"

Well, as you can imagine, instead of having hunting dog dreams on the way home, I had to listen to Zeke's barking as he proceeded to tell Sly his side of the calf story. He wanted to make sure she understood we didn't have proper training from our hunters. I did notice that Sly was yawning and trying to sleep while Zeke kept barking. Maybe my little brother really didn't have a full understanding of his problem with the calf. I decided this was not the right time to tell Zeke about my story, so I simply nodded from time to time when Zeke looked my way. Sometimes it was best for my little brother to figure things out on his own. After all, I believed Sly liked me best!

CHAPTER 9

The Upside-Down Owl

THE GREAT HORNED OWL

This is what we hunting dogs call "the off season." It simply means we don't hunt during this season. The birds need to rest and repopulate.

The real truth concerning the off season is quite simple. Our hunter told us the truth. He said, "Doc, I'm really sorry we can't go hunting until next season, but you know how the queen gets. She saves up all the outside work for me during the hunting season so that I will have plenty to do in the off season."

We know the queen as the other one. She is just

another one of those people. She is not a hunter and not like the great one. So when we are not hunting, we pretty much lay around sleeping, eating, and chasing squirrels and birds.

Now you know a little about the off season. And during that time, I enjoy another form of activity, one that involves my unusual friend, a great horned owl. We have an agreement. The owl perches himself on top of the swing set so that he can protect the people's vegetable garden from other birds and animals—all except for me. He looks the other way when I pull tomatoes off the vines and eat them. In return, I don't bark or chase after him.

I feel bad because our people are always trying to find out what happens to all those tomatoes. But what can I say? I love eating juicy tomatoes.

One morning my son, Rush, barked, "Pa, come quick! Our owl is upside down!

PREDICAMENT

I ran to the swing set. Sure enough, the owl hung upside down with his talons (claws) clasped tightly around the trapeze bar, which was on the end of the swing set. His brown feathered body swayed back and forth in the wind. The owl's ear tufts looked like two short legs sticking out from his round yellow eyes. He didn't look well at all.

"Owl," I said. "What happened?"

Blinking, the owl turned his head toward me. "Doc, it's a mystery to me. I was perched on this swing set, thinking about how I would like to have a real name like you. Everybody calls me Owl. Zeke told me the other day that the name Owl was just too common. He felt any animal at the Lazy Dog Hacienda ought to have a proper name, something you could put on those papers he's always barking about. You know, the pedigree papers. As I was thinking about names, suddenly I was upside down! I thought the sky and the ground had changed places. When both of you appeared upside down, I realized it must be me."

I answered calmly as I scratched behind my ears. "Don't worry. I think I know how we'll get you out of this predicament. First, Rush and I will get Newt to help. Hang on tight, and we'll be right back!"

The great horned owl continued to sway back and forth while hooting, "Make it soon. I'm getting dizzy."

Rush and I barked for Newt, running to the barn. Newt, the black Lab in our family, was crouched down in the blue-stem grass in the north pasture. For some reason, Newt never liked coyotes. He would patiently wait for the neighborhood coyotes to come around so that he could bark and scare them away.

"Newt," I barked. "We have a horrible predicament! The owl is upside down. We need your help … right now!"

"I'll help. I'll help. You know I will." Newt stood up and immediately started wagging his tail. Newt's tail hit Rush right in the face back and forth. *Whack, whack.*

Almost falling down, Rush yelled, "Newt, stop that. You are hitting me in the head with your long tail!"

"I'm really sorry, Rush. Truly I am." With that said, Newt sat down on his haunches (back end). "Doc, what does predicament mean?"

"Well," I barked as loud as I could, "predicament means a problem that is considered a bad situation. Owl is upside down and needs to be right side up."

Just then we heard some loud hooting and squawking coming from owl. The three of us ran back to Owl and the swing set.

Poor Owl. He looked even worse. He whispered something about the blood going to his head. Owl was becoming so weak that he now was hanging on the trapeze bar with only one of his talons.

I told Newt to lie down under the trapeze bar. Then in my most confident of barking voices, I stated, "Owl, let go, and you will fall right on Newt's back. That'll give you a soft landing. When I bark once, you let go." Owl nodded yes and waited for me to bark. As soon as owl's body swung directly over Newt, I barked. Owl let go and landed safely on Newt. Fortunately for us, Newt weighed more than eighty pounds. He was rather large, so it actually would have been hard for Owl to miss the mark.

Owl hooted in joy. Rush and Newt barked happily. And I had just saved Owl. Or so I thought.

PROBLEM SOLVED?

Later that day I heard a strange noise. *"Aw-choo, aw-choo, aw-chooo,"* Owl hooted as he turned upside down again on the same trapeze bar as before. Rush and I were taking our afternoon siesta (sleeping) close to the swing set.

"Rush," I barked. "Get Newt again. Owl's swinging on the bar."

"Okay, Pa." Rush starting running. "I'll get him. He's stalking mice in the south pasture."

Newt loved to bring mice back to our people. He always felt the people enjoyed the mice, especially when they screamed as he dropped them in the swimming pool while they swam.

I tried to calm Owl while we waited on Rush and Newt. Owl was very upset. "Doc, I'm getting tired of seeing everything upside down."

Scratching my ear, I replied, "When did you notice you were upside down again?"

It was hard for the owl to talk. The blood in his body now sat in his two ear tufts. "I guess it would be when I sneezed," Owl hooted weakly while he took a deep breath. "Doc, you know I don't do this when I'm not sneezing." Then Owl let out a long sigh.

I looked at Owl seriously. "That's it. Don't you see? I've solved the problem! Sneezing causes you to turn upside down on your perch. When you don't sneeze, you don't fall over!"

"Why, Doc, you are so smart. But what am I going to do about it? I can't stop myself from sneezing." Saying this was almost too much for Owl.

"Hmmmm! That's another problem," I said as I saw Newt and Rush coming toward us. Newt once again lay down under the trapeze bar, and on my bark, Owl plopped down on Newt. Owl was saved again, at least as long as he didn't sneeze.

PROBLEM REALLY SOLVED!

A few weeks later, Rush, Newt, and I were taking a siesta near the swing set again, and Owl was perched on the big trapeze bar. The wind really started blowing.

Startled, I awoke to the hooting sounds of *aw-choo, aw-choo, aw-choooo.* I stood up on all fours and saw owl once again swinging back and forth upside down on the trapeze bar.

"Doc, I just can't take this anymore. I started sneezing, and now I'm upside down again. What are we going to do? An owl can't live upside down all the time. What will all the other owls think?" Just as Owl finished saying that, Newt quickly moved under the trapeze bar, and Owl plopped down on Newt. Owl was saved again. However, that didn't solve our predicament.

I scratched really hard behind my ears. Then it came to me. All three times one of us was near Owl when he started sneezing. The people always talked about how some of their friends were allergic to dog hair. That had to be it. Owl was allergic to our dog hair. "Owl," I barked, "you are allergic to our dog hair, especially when the wind blows. It blows the dog hair directly toward you!"

Owl squawked as he flew back on the swing set, "Doc, what can I do? It is always windy in Oklahoma. We can't do anything about that. And you are my family and my best friends! I like having you around."

"Aha," I replied. "There is something we can do. We can scratch downwind."

"Great," Owl hooted. "But what can I do?"

I barked loudly. "You will have to fly off your perch every time you think you're going to sneeze!"

THE GREAT HORNED OWL GETS A NAME

I kept thinking about what Owl said about wanting a name. Now that our predicament concerning Owl and the swing set was solved, we could concentrate on a name for him. Rush, Newt, and I met around the walnut tree trunk to have a naming rights meeting. Since I was the oldest and wisest, I sat on the stump. I barked, "Owl doesn't have any people to name him, so it's up to us to find a good name for him. We should name him something that is personal only to Owl."

We all thought and thought. Finally, I barked, "What about Sneezy? That's a perfect name for owl since he sneezes all the time. Raise your right front paw if you agree." Everyone agreed.

Sneezy likes his name. He doesn't have any more trouble on the swing set. Before a sneeze, he flies to the garden, where he now spends so much time that the animals and insects stay away.

Rush, Newt, and I scratch downwind as much as possible. They both think I'm pretty smart since I solved Sneezy's problem.

I continue to compliment Sneezy on taking care of the garden. Our people continue looking for answers to the mystery of the missing tomatoes. And I still sneak a ripe red tomato or two and wait patiently for hunting season.

ABOUT THE AUTHOR

Linda Harkey has been an enthusiastic hunting dog owner for more than thirty years. As a docent, she has been involved with the writing of curricula for children's programs at local museums. Harkey is also the author of a children's book, *The Budding Staff*. She lives with her husband and dogs on twenty acres in Catoosa, Oklahoma.

The inspirations for this book

Printed in the United States
By Bookmasters